Riy...

Fast, brave, impulsive. She never lets a silly thing like rules stand in her way.

Sam

Extremely tall and extremely clumsy, but when it comes to spying, he's the best.

The Voids

Robotic spiders set on destroying the Night Zoo and plunging it into darkness.

This book was co-written by Giles Clare

OXFORD
UNIVERSITY PRESS

Great Clarendon Street, Oxford OX2 6DP

Oxford University Press is a department of the University of Oxford.
It furthers the University's objective of excellence in research, scholarship,
and education by publishing worldwide. Oxford is a registered trade mark of
Oxford University Press in the UK and in certain other countries

First published 2018

British Library Cataloguing in Publication Data

Data available

ISBN: 978-0-19-276406-5

1 3 5 7 9 10 8 6 4 2

Printed in Great Britain

Paper used in the production of this book is a natural,
recyclable product made from wood grown in sustainable forests.
The manufacturing process conforms to the environmental
regulations of the country of origin.

NIGHT ZOO KEEPER

The Lioness of Fire Desert

Joshua Davidson

Illustrated by
Buzz Burman

OXFORD
UNIVERSITY PRESS

Chapter One

Will Rivers the Night Zookeeper, together with Riya and Sam the Spying Giraffe, passed through the magical portal. Seconds before, they had said goodbye to the other giraffes and the lush coolness of the Whispering Woods. Now the three friends were standing in the fierce heat of the Fire Desert. Will felt his feet sinking into the fine sand.

He could feel the warmth of it through his shoes. Sweat was already beading on his forehead. 'Wow, it's like stepping into an oven,' remarked Riya.

'Ouch, my hooves are burning,' grumbled Sam. 'Phff, phffff!' He lifted one front leg off the ground and blew on his hoof. Off-balance, the young giraffe wobbled and quickly shoved his hoof back down. Straight on top of Riya's foot.

'Ow!' she complained. 'Why are you so clumsy?'

Will was taking in their environment. They were surrounded by sand, from low, snaking ripples to towering dunes, stretching out endlessly in all directions. Surprisingly, they were also surrounded by water.

Hundreds of silvery lakes, each reflecting the full moon, sat between the dunes. Many of the lakes were fringed by palm trees, but at the heart of each one was a swirling jet of flames as tall as a tree.

A recent memory blazed in Will's mind. The flames reminded him of the candles on his birthday cake. He thought for a moment.

So much had happened since he had sneaked off from home: entering the Night Zoo; meeting Sam; being rescued by Riya; and helping to save the giraffes from those terrible Voids. And now, he was here, in the middle of this magnificent, forbidding desert with a job to do: he was the new Night Zookeeper. Except, he still didn't really know what that meant. No one had left any instructions.

He took off his hat to wipe his forehead. He looked at the metal badge on the peak of the hat. It was the same shape as the purple elephant he had painted on the zoo wall and for some reason he thought of his Grandma Rivers. Will sighed. He suddenly really missed her. He missed all his family, even his scruffy little brother. He missed home.

'What's up, Will?' asked Riya.

'Those flames. They're like the candles on my birthday cake,' said Will.

'Must have been a big cake,' said Sam. Will smiled weakly and the giraffe continued, 'Hey, Riya, did you know I get heartburn every time

I eat birthday cake?'

Riya shook her head. 'That's a shame,' she replied.

Sam gave her a goofy smile. 'Yeah, so the doctor told me next time, take the candles off first!'

Riya rolled her eyes and groaned.

'What's the matter? You got a stomach-cake?' asked Sam. 'Geddit? Stomach-cake? Stomach-ache?'

'Argh, Will, can you make him stop?' said Riya.

7

'Sam, can you help?' asked Will. 'What can you see from up there?'

Sam raised his head as high as he could and peered around. 'Nothing really. Just sand and lakes and those twisty fiery thingies.'

Will turned to Riya. 'Which way do you think we should go? There are animals in trouble here, but I don't know where.'

Riya shrugged. 'Maybe you should try the Orb.'

'Wait a minute; there is something over there,' said Sam, squinting. 'It looks like . . . a big metal creature.'

A tingle of fear fizzed up Will's spine as he

recalled their recent battles in the Whispering Woods. 'Metal?' he repeated. 'It's not a Void, is it?'

'Not unless it's grown wings,' said Sam. 'And a moustache.'

'Huh?' said Will. 'What's it doing? Is it moving?'

'Not exactly. It's just sort of bobbing.'

'Bobbing?' replied Riya, baffled.

'Yes, on a lake. Oh, hang on. No, now it's twirling its moustache. Wow, look at it go!'

'Sam, are you feeling alright?' asked Will. 'You're not making much sense.'

'Oh, strange, it's stopped again,' noted Sam.

Riya suddenly put her face in her hands and groaned. Will looked alarmed. 'Riya? What's wrong?'

'I'm fine; I'm fine,' Riya replied with a wry smile. 'I know what it is. The metal creature.' She called up to Sam. 'Hey, Sam, have you never seen an aeroplane before? Or to be more precise, a seaplane?'

'What? Yes. I mean, of course I've seen a . . . a plane before. Who hasn't?' he replied with a nervous laugh.

Riya looked at him suspiciously. 'Is that

why you think its propeller
is a moustache?' she
scoffed.

'A plane!' exclaimed Will.
'Sam, pick me up so I can see,
will you?' Sam clamped his
teeth on the collar of Will's
coat and lifted him onto his
back. Will grimaced as he felt
warm dribble stream down the
back of his neck. He wrapped his
arms around the giraffe's neck
to steady himself. Will stared
out across the desert

landscape. There was a flash of silver in the distance. There *was* a plane. An old silver seaplane was sitting next to the shore of a large lake.

Will felt hot breath on his ear. 'Will,' whispered Sam. 'Um, quick question.' The giraffe glanced down quickly at Riya.

'Yes?' Will whispered back.

'Will, what's a plane?' asked the giraffe.

Will smiled. 'I guessed you didn't know,' he replied under his breath.

'I've never left the Whispering Woods before,' explained Sam, sounding a bit embarrassed.

'It's alright,' Will said. 'What's a plane?

Well, that's a plane and it might just be our ticket out of here. You were right, Riya. It's an old seaplane.'

Riya nodded with satisfaction. 'Knew it!'

Will suddenly noticed the plane's propeller jerk and begin to rotate slowly. Thick smoke belched out of the sides of the nose. The whole plane shuddered as the propeller whirled up to speed. Seconds later, however, the engine spluttered to a halt again.

'No!' Will exclaimed. 'The moustache—I mean the propeller—is turning. Someone's trying to start the engine. We need to get down there before they leave!'

At that moment, there was a painfully loud screech of metal behind them. Sam was startled and Will toppled from his perch. He landed on his hands and knees in the soft sand. His heart was already pumping in his chest. Although Will couldn't see the danger yet, he had heard that terrible sound before. He whipped off his backpack and drew out his torch.

The skyline at the top of the dune glowed red and then a grey, metal head appeared. Will gasped as the robot spider crested the top of the dune. This Void was bigger, much bigger and more menacing than the ones they had defeated in the woods. The giant robot halted and fixed its crimson eye on Will. His hand shaking, Will lifted the torch to aim it at the Void.

'Let it have it!' cried Riya. 'The light will drive that monster away!'

Will gritted his teeth and held the switch down. The torch rattled in his grip and a brilliant beam of light burst across the dune straight at the metal spider. To Will's astonishment, the Void didn't flinch. There was a soft hiss and a feeble puff of smoke as light struck metal, but the Void ignored it. Instead, it narrowed its red eye and advanced.

'I don't understand,' said Will. 'The torch. It's not working like before.' A pulse of fear raced along his limbs.

'Then we definitely need to get down there before that plane leaves!' said Riya.

'Run for it!' shouted Will.

Will, Sam and Riya charged down the slope of the dune, stumbling and slipping on the sand. Will's heart was racing and his lungs were hungry for air. He glanced over his shoulder. The Void was chasing them. Will couldn't believe the torch beam had not affected the giant robot. Fortunately, the Void seemed to be struggling in the soft conditions too: its long, pointy legs were sinking deep into the sand under its enormous weight.

'This way!' shouted Sam, keeping his eyes fixed on the large lake.

'Is the plane still there?' gasped Riya. 'It hasn't taken off yet, has it?'

'No, it's still there,' Sam replied and then added, 'Sorry, what do you mean? Taken off?'

'I thought you knew what a plane was!' replied Riya. 'What do you think the wings are for? It takes off. It flies. Up in the air. Where we're going to get away from that robot!'

Sam's dark eyes flew wide open. 'But I can't

fly!' he protested. 'I'm scared of heights!'

'What kind of giraffe is scared of heights?' cried Riya in disbelief.

Will looked back again. He almost smiled as he noted that the Void was losing ground. It was hissing in frustration as it became bogged down. 'Please stop arguing and keep going,' Will urged the others.

A few minutes later, they rounded a dune, and Will spotted the seaplane on the lake ahead of them. He could also make out a figure in the cockpit.

'My ossicones are tingling,' announced Sam. 'That Void must be catching up!'

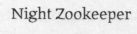

'That doesn't make sense,' said Riya, looking back. 'We're getting further away.'

Will peered into the cockpit. There was definitely someone there. Will felt a rush of hope. 'There's a person inside! A pilot!' he shouted and waved his arms frantically. 'Hey! Hey! Pilot, help! Start the plane!'

Sam suddenly skidded to a halt. Will and Riya stopped and looked back at him. 'Sam! What are you doing? Come on. That Void's still coming!' said Will.

Sam was staring at the cockpit of the plane. The colour had drained from his face and his eyes were bright and glistening. 'That's not a person, Will,' the giraffe replied with a gulp. Will swivelled round to look at the plane. 'That's why my ossicones were warning me.'

The figure threw open the cockpit window and a golden-brown face emerged. 'That's a lioness!' exclaimed the giraffe.

From across the lake, Will heard a rumbling, angry roar. The lioness pilot was baring her huge canine teeth and shaking a clenched paw at them. She ducked her head back inside the cockpit and frantically fiddled with the controls. The propeller began to rotate in fits and starts and smoke belched from the engine exhausts.

'Look! She must have heard me,' said Will. 'Come on, Sam!'

Sam's legs were shaking violently. 'You want me to fly?' he said forlornly. 'In a metal bird?

With a lion?'

'No choice, Sam,' said Will firmly. 'But to be safe, you might want to use that invisibility trick of yours.' Sam nodded eagerly and closed his eyes in concentration. The outline of the young giraffe's body began to glow until suddenly he became transparent and disappeared from sight.

As they approached the seaplane, the lioness pilot stuck her head out of the window again and shook her paw. The engine was coughing and popping, and Will could barely make out what she was shouting: 'Grrr, stay back! Keep away from my plane! Grrr!'

Will and Riya pulled up on the shore next to the plane. Invisible Sam stood a few paces behind them, still quivering. 'Please help us!' Will called out. 'We're being chased.' Will pointed back along the shore. At that very moment, the giant Void lumbered into view. Its red eye was glowing furiously.

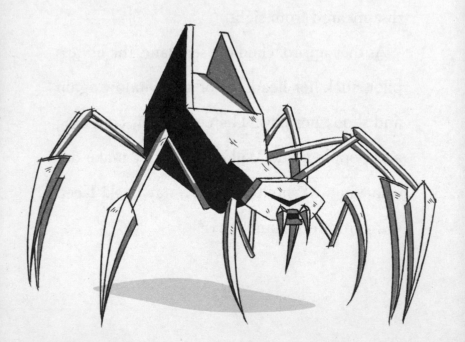

The lioness pilot turned to face them. Will immediately noticed an old wound on her face: a deep scar as straight as a ruler ran across her wide nose and down her jowl. Will realized immediately that he had been wrong. She wasn't angry; her amber eyes were full of fear. 'Leave me alone!' the lioness said. 'Go somewhere else. Why did you lead it here?'

Riya pleaded, 'You're our only chance.'

The lioness was staring wide-eyed at the approaching Void. 'No, I can't help you. I've got to go,' she said softly.

Suddenly, Will felt himself being hoisted into the air by the scruff of the neck. Unseen by the lioness, Sam lifted Will directly onto the plane's wing.

The lioness swung round and roared, 'No! There isn't time.'

'Please let us in!' said Will, clambering forwards towards the cockpit. Behind him, Sam deposited Riya on the wing.

The lioness glanced at the two children and then at the Void and then threw her paws up in the air. 'Alright, alright, get in!' she growled. She reached over and threw open the cockpit door. Will and Riya slipped and slid across the smooth wing towards the inside of the seaplane.

Chapter Two

'**F**aster, Will,' urged Riya. She was first to reach the door. 'The Void. It's here!' Riya tumbled onto the floor behind the pilots' seats. She spun round to grab Will's arm and pull him inside to safety. She was just too late. Crimson light flooded the interior of the plane. Riya saw a flash of silvery-grey metal as a long leg loomed over the wing. It struck the side of the seaplane. There was a hideous, screeching noise as the Void's spiked foot scraped across the fuselage. Will paused for half a second to cover his ears. It was a mistake. He cried out in pain as the Void's foot slashed the back of his leg. He staggered into the aircraft and grabbed his calf with both hands. Suddenly, there was a loud crack and pop as the Void's leg shattered one of the windows. Riya yelped with surprise as they were showered in an explosion of tiny pieces of glass. In pain, Will backed himself up against the wall next to Riya and hugged his knees to his chest. 'My leg,' he said through gritted teeth. 'The Void caught me.'

Riya looked up at the lioness in the pilot's seat. To her dismay, the lioness wasn't moving. She wasn't attempting to start the engine. Their pilot was hunched over, clinging on to the control stick. Riya could hear her mumbling.

'No, not again,' the lioness was saying. 'This can't be happening.' Riya scrambled to her feet and threw herself into the seat next to the pilot. She could see the lioness' whiskers were trembling.

'Hey!' Riya said. 'Snap out of it! Start the engine!'

'I never wanted to see that thing again,' the lioness moaned. 'There's no escape this time.'

Outside the Void hissed and gnashed its fangs together. Clicker clacker! Clicker clacker! Glossy tar was dribbling from its fangs into the lake water. The Void reached out and pressed a spiked foot onto the wing. The seaplane rocked.

'Listen, you've got to start the engine,' insisted Riya. 'My friend is injured. That monster just hurt him.' She reached out and gently ran a fingertip along the scar on the lioness' nose. The pilot flinched in surprise. 'Like it hurt you,' said Riya softly.

The lioness' amber eyes suddenly blazed into life. She raised her head and roared with anger. Immediately, the lioness took hold of the control stick and started to flick switches and push and pull stoppers. 'I'll get your friend out of here,' she growled. 'But I need your help.'

'Of course,' nodded Riya. 'Just tell me what to do.'

'The engine. It keeps starting and stopping. The propeller is jammed. It needs an extra push,' the lioness said.

Riya didn't hesitate. She jumped up and threw open the cockpit door on the opposite side to the Void.

'Riya, what are you doing?' Will called out. 'You can't go—'

But Riya was already out on the wing. She stepped towards the front edge and climbed on top of the plane's nose. She could hear Will's muffled shouts of protest from inside: 'Riya, come back in. It's too dangerous.' Riya's heart was thudding steadily under her ribs as she gracefully got to her feet. She fixed her eyes on the propeller a few feet ahead and took a light step towards it. The Void must have spotted her because she heard an angry hiss and the seaplane lurched up and down violently. Riya almost toppled off the side, but she pounced forwards and wrapped her arms around one of the propeller blades. Below her, she could see the clear lake water was changing: the Void Gunk was turning it grey and greasy. The plane bucked again. This time Riya's feet slipped from under her, and she slid halfway down the blade still clinging to it. She tried to stand up, but her shoes wouldn't grip on the smooth engine casing. She hung onto the propeller, but she realized that it would only take one more strike: if the Void shook the plane again, she would be tipped into the stinking, polluted water below.

Just at that moment, she heard Sam's voice ring out: 'Oi! Over here, you ugly robot!'

'Sam, no!' Will called out hoarsely. 'Stay away!'

Riya glanced towards the shore. Her heart leapt. She couldn't see the giraffe. Sam was still invisible.

'Yeah, you heard me!' called out Invisible Sam. 'Over here!'

Riya watched as the Void lowered its legs away from the plane and scuttled around on the shore, searching for Sam. Riya understood what to do. Sam had bought her a few short seconds of time. She hauled herself to her feet and put both hands on the propeller blade. She turned back to the cockpit.

'Ready!' she shouted.

The pilot lioness nodded and punched the starter button. The powerful engine whirred and clanked beneath Riya's feet. 'Wait. Wait . . . now!' ordered the lioness.

Riya shoved down hard on the blade. It twitched, but didn't budge. She glanced back in concern at the lioness, who was adjusting some controls. 'Again. Now!' roared the pilot. Riya took a deep breath and wrenched down on the blade with all her strength.

Immediately, the engine shook as it fired

into life. Riya coughed as she was engulfed in a plume of smoke. The propeller jerked into action, and the air was filled with a deafening buzz as it spun up to speed.

'Yes, Riya!' shouted Will. Riya leapt off the nose back onto the wing.

There was a loud splash and the seaplane lurched on its floats.

'Watch out!' Sam warned.

The Void had abandoned its search for Sam, rushed into the lake and reached over the fuselage with one of its long legs. Riya barely had time to sway out of the way as one of the Void's spiked feet swished past her face. In doing so, she slipped and slid rapidly down the wing past the door. She flipped onto her front and grabbed at the smooth metal. Just as her feet and legs tipped over the edge, Riya's fingers caught on the wing flap. Half dangling in the air, Riya clung for her life above the filthy grey water.

The engine throbbed and the propeller hummed even louder as the lioness opened the throttles. The seaplane juddered forward and the lioness began to turn the seaplane away from the shore. 'Riya!' Will called out. Riya saw Will leaning out of the door.

She let go of the flap with one hand and grasped Will's outstretched arm. Will pulled as hard as he could and Riya managed to clamber back up onto the wing. The Void's foot swiped viciously at her again, but she ducked under it and dived into the plane.

'Hold on to something,' ordered the lioness and opened the throttles to the maximum, even though the plane was still turning. Will caught a glimpse of the Void through the smashed window. It was towering up on its back legs, black tar spurting from its fangs.

It was about to smash its entire weight down on them. At that moment, the tail of the seaplane swung round wildly. The fin smacked into the Void's exposed underbelly. Will gasped in surprise as he saw several thick bolts fly off. A large armoured plate dropped off the Void and crashed into the lake. The Void staggered back onto the shore, hissing and squealing, and then it disappeared from view as the seaplane rose on its floats and accelerated faster and faster across the water. The lioness pilot pulled back on the stick and the seaplane lifted clear of the lake and into the air. But there was something wrong. The plane bumped and twitched, and the lioness had to fight the controls to fly straight and level.

'I don't get it. She's flying heavy,' she complained. 'It's as if we've got some extra cargo.'

Will and Riya exchanged glances.

'I think I might know why,' Will said. 'Hold this a sec.' He passed his zookeeper cap to Riya and hobbled over to the missing window. He eased the top of his head through the hole. The air whipped his hair into his face as he peeked up at the top of the seaplane. For a second, Will was alarmed. And then there was a flash of light and Sam the Sying Giraffe

43

became visible again. Sam was lying on top of the seaplane, clinging to the fuselage with his long legs. He had his eyes screwed shut and his ears flat against his head.

'Sam, are you okay?' Will shouted.

Sam opened one eye, peeked out and promptly closed it again. 'Noooooo!' he wailed. 'I don't like it!'

Riya poked her head out next to Will. 'Could be worse,' shouted Riya above the roar of the air.

'What? What could possibly be worse?' cried Sam and moaned miserably.

'At least you're not in here with the lioness!' she replied.

Chapter Three

The lioness called back over her shoulder, 'You two had better sit down.' She was still struggling with the controls to keep the seaplane steady.

Riya helped to support Will as he limped to the front of the cockpit. He lowered himself gingerly into the other pilot's seat.

'I'm Claw,' said the lioness. 'I'm captain of

this old seaplane, Le Canard.'

'Pleased to meet you, Captain Claw,' replied Riya. 'I'm Riya. This is Will. And your extra passenger on the roof is Sam.'

Will whispered to Riya, 'What did she say the plane's called?'

'Le Canard,' she whispered back. 'It means The Duck.'

Unexpectedly, Will felt a burst of irritation. How did Riya know that? How come she seemed to know everything? He thought about how brave she had just been starting the engine while he had been stuck uselessly in the cockpit. She had been the real hero while he had let that Void catch him. He should have felt grateful and full of admiration. Instead, he turned his face away, frowning. He was the Night Zookeeper. Wasn't he supposed to be the hero? A feeling of gloom was seeping into his thoughts, spreading like the venom from a snake bite. As if to remind him of his failure, the pain from his wound suddenly flared up. He tried not to groan, but he couldn't stop himself.

Captain Claw looked away from the controls for a second to examine Will's leg. 'We need to get you to a hospital,' she announced. 'The sooner you get treated, the quicker we can stop the effects spreading. I should know.'

Will stared out of the windscreen in front of him. The Fire Desert stretched out on all sides. He could see hundreds of flickering flames marking the lakes. It would have been a magical sight, but the throbbing pain in his leg made the landscape feel endless and hostile. He peeked down at his lower leg. To his horror, he noticed that his skin was pale and sweaty. No, not pale, he decided. It was grey. 'Is the hospital far?' he asked quietly.

'Not far,' replied the lioness. 'It's at the Great Pink Lake. Let's just hope we get there before any of those robots do.'

'Voids, you mean!' said Will. 'You've seen more of them?'

Captain Claw nodded grimly. 'Oh yes. Lots. Not just here in the Fire Desert. They're everywhere in the Night Zoo.'

Will swallowed. Everywhere! The Night Zoo was overrun by Voids. And he was supposed to save it? He grimaced as pain shot up his leg. He felt weak. 'Don't bother,' he mumbled. 'Forget the hospital. Can you take me to the zoo gates? I want to go home.'

'Take it easy. We're going to get you some help,' Riya said.

Will shook his head. 'No, take me home!' he

snapped. 'What's the point of staying here? I can't save the Night Zoo from all those Voids. I'm useless.'

'What's the matter with you?' Riya asked. 'Stop talking like that.'

'It's not his fault,' said Captain Claw. 'The wound is small, but the infection is spreading to his mind, dragging him down. We need to hurry.' She thumped on the ceiling and shouted, 'Hey, giraffe! You still up there?'

'Unfortunately, yes!' came the muffled reply. 'Flying's horrible. And dangerous.'

'Nonsense,' called out Captain Claw with a smirk. 'Flying isn't dangerous. Crashing is dangerous!'

'Not funny!' cried Sam.

'Listen up, you giant wing-walker. You need to hang on tight. This could be a bumpy landing.'

The lioness banked the seaplane hard to the right.

'Whoa, make it stop!' moaned Sam. 'I want to get off!'

'Just a few more minutes, Sam,' Riya called out.

Suddenly, the plane jolted and wobbled in the air. Riya felt her stomach rise in her chest. Captain Claw steadied the stick and shouted irritably, 'Keep still, would you? You're going to make me lose control.'

'I can't help it!' shouted Sam. 'My hooves are slipping!' The plane bucked and shuddered again as if they were flying through sudden turbulence. 'Help!' cried Sam.

The nose of the plane suddenly rose. Riya stumbled backwards as the seaplane began to climb steeply. She grabbed the window frame and peered out. 'Oh no!' she whispered. Sam wasn't on top of the plane anymore. Now, the poor young giraffe was hanging by his front hooves from the tail fin!

Captain Claw pushed hard on the stick to try to point the nose down, but the extra weight on the tail was too much. The plane began to slow and stall. She pushed the throttles fully forward and the engine roared in protest.

'That lanky fool of a giraffe,' cursed Captain Claw. 'He's going to make us crash.'

'Hey, that's my friend,' Riya replied crossly. 'He helped us escape, remember?' She shot forwards and stood beside the lioness. 'Let me help,' she said and placed her hands on the stick below the lioness' paws. They both shoved the stick forwards and slowly the plane broke out of its dangerous climb. The nose dropped below the horizon and the seaplane began to descend.

'There!' said Captain Claw, pointing at a large lake ahead. 'The Great Pink Lake!'

In the other pilot's seat, Will was glumly

examining his injured leg. The grey colour had spread from his knee to his ankle. Despite all the drama inside and outside the plane, he felt as if it were all happening to someone else. Almost as if he were watching some action movie on TV. His heart was beating slowly and his breathing steady. He felt no sense of excitement or danger. In fact, he just felt empty. He glanced up at the great body of

water and saw jets of swirling flames at the centre of the lake. Strangely, the flames weren't orange, or red, or even pink. They looked grey like his leg. 'Doesn't look very pink to me,' he grunted and then he realized that he didn't really care.

Between them, Captain Claw and Riya managed to put the plane into an emergency dive. 'That's it,' said Claw with gritted teeth.

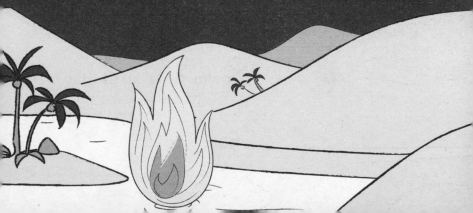

'Keep her steady.' The plane rocked and swayed like a drunk bumblebee.

'Why are you going faster?' cried Sam, his back legs twirling behind him. As he spoke, the air caught his long, wet tongue and slapped it back and forth across his face. 'Thtupid tung! Thtop it!' he mumbled.

The seaplane arced down towards the huge lake. Riya felt her ears popping. She spotted some lights amongst the palm trees at the far

58

end of the lake. Claw nodded. 'The hospital,' she said with a grim smile. 'Help me pull the nose up for landing.'

'Hey, what's that?' asked Will indifferently. Out of nowhere, a rolling bank of thick grey smoke was rising rapidly from the lake surface.

'Up and over!' barked Captain Claw, but it was too late. Within seconds, the seaplane was swallowed up by the monstrous, suffocating smoke.

'Oo thurned out de lighths?' shouted Sam, his tongue flapping noisily against his cheek.

Flying blind, the lioness fixed her eyes on the instrument panel, checking the height and speed. 'We're coming in hard and fast,' she warned.

Just as suddenly, the seaplane shot out of the cloud. The grey surface of the lake filled the entire windscreen. Claw and Riya wrenched back on the stick and Le Canard's nose lifted. With incredible skill, the lioness levelled the seaplane out, throttled back the power and the two floats skimmed across the smooth water. But Le Canard didn't settle. It bounced off the surface and up again. 'Too fast, too fast!' muttered Claw. 'We need to slow down.'

Riya looked up at the lights and palm trees ahead. They were getting rapidly closer. 'Sam!'

she shouted.

'What!'

'Put your feet down,' she ordered.

'What?'

'Just do it!' she urged.

Still hanging onto the tail, Sam tucked his back legs underneath him and lowered his feet. His hooves kissed the water. 'Wheee!' he cried. Riya glanced out of the window and almost laughed: Sam the Spying Giraffe was water-skiing gracefully behind the plane. 'Now this I like! This is much more fun than flying,' he called out to her. 'Wheee!'

With Sam helping to slow their speed, the

seaplane finally touched down on the lake and bumped across the grey water on its floats. Captain Claw cut the power, but Le Canard continued to skid uncontrollably towards the shore.

'Uh-oh,' said Will quietly as the palm trees loomed into view.

Claw roared in alarm. 'We're out of lake! Brace yourselves!'

There was a terrible jolt as the seaplane struck the shore and skidded up the beach.

At the top of the bank, the plane's nose arrowed between two swaying palm trees. And then their ride finally came to a crunching halt as the poor plane's wings crumpled into the two trees.

Chapter Four

Captain Claw opened the cockpit door and leapt to the ground. 'My plane!' she howled.

The crash had shaken Will out of his dark, detached mood. 'What happened? Where are we?' he asked Riya.

'Hospital,' she replied and helped Will clamber down the plane's crumpled wing.

Sam was standing up to his knees in the lake. 'Did you see me?' he asked excitedly. 'Did you see me water-skiing? It's the one thing I'm not clumsy at.'

Captain Claw ignored him and stared mournfully at the seaplane's smashed wings. She shook her head and said, 'Look at my beautiful aeroplane!'

'More like an error plane,' said Sam with a goofy grin. Captain Claw narrowed her amber eyes and growled at him menacingly. Sam's smile disappeared. 'Too soon?' he asked. Riya and Claw both nodded. 'Okay, too soon. Sorry.'

'Er, you guys,' said Will. He had limped away from the plane towards the lights. 'We've got company.'

A small group of animals was standing in a line nearby, staring wide-eyed at the crash scene. Each one had an instrument. There was a fox with a flute, a vole with a tiny violin, and a cheetah with a cello. A tubby tapir with a tuba had his lips pressed to the mouthpiece. He must have been holding his breath because suddenly he breathed out. The tuba made a long wet parping noise.

'That's disgusting!' said Sam and wrinkled his nose.

'We came to play you a welcome tune, but . . . that,' said the fox, pointing at the ruined seaplane.

By now, other animals were gathering behind the band. A few shouts of surprise and excitement went up:

'Look, it's him. He's here!'

'Who? Where? Let me through.'

'It is! The new Night Zookeeper has arrived!'

'He's come to save us.'

Will shook his head wearily. No, not this again, he thought.

'Save us from the Fog.'

'And save us from the Grip!'

A moan of fear swept through the crowd.

'The Grip! The Grip!'

There was a sudden flurry of neon pink feathers as a bird twirled in the air above the crowd. The beautiful flamingo flapped her

68

wings and landed neatly between the crowd and Will.

'Hello, Night Zookeeper,' she said. 'I am Doctor Florence Flamingo. I am honoured to meet you.'

'Hi,' replied Will.

'And welcome back, Captain,' said Florence. 'I'm sorry about your plane.'

Captain Claw was shaking her head. 'I couldn't stop her, Florence. She just skimmed over the water like a skipping stone.'

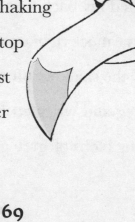

The crowd of animals moaned in unison again.

'The Grip! The Grip has polluted the water. Nobody go near the water!'

There was a sudden silence as all eyes turned to stare at Sam. The giraffe's dark, hooded eyes flew open in alarm. He lifted a front leg out of the water. His hoof and shin were covered in thick grey sludge. The crowd groaned. Sam inspected his back legs. They were covered in the same muck right up to his tail. Sam galloped out of the shallows on to the beach. He shook each leg and wriggled his backside vigorously, spraying blobs of grey gunk everywhere.

'Hey, watch out!' cried the tapir with the tuba.

Sam stopped shaking. 'That's a bit better,' he said, but his legs and coat were still dirty. His eyelids drooped and his knees wobbled.

'Sam?' said Will. 'What's the matter?' Will's head was still clearing, but he could tell that there was something wrong with his friend.

'I don't feel so good,' the young giraffe said weakly.

Doctor Florence looked concerned. 'Sam, I need to clean you up properly,' she said. 'Can you follow me to the hospital?'

Sam nodded and staggered forwards sleepily. Will started to limp back towards his friend, but his injured leg collapsed beneath him. He went down on one knee and cried out in pain.

'You're hurt too!' exclaimed Florence in surprise. She looked down at Will's leg with her sharp, yellow eyes. 'Why didn't you say? What happened?'

'It was a giant robotic spider. It scratched me,' said Will, wincing.

'Will, listen. This is important. Tell me exactly how you've been feeling,' Florence ordered.

'Kind of strange,' replied Will truthfully. 'A bit useless. Empty. We were going to crash and I didn't really care.'

Doctor Florence shook her head. 'Then you need immediate treatment too.' She turned to the crowd behind her. 'What were you all doing?' she scolded them. 'You should be ashamed of yourselves. The Night Zookeeper is hurt and you've been wasting time moaning about the Grip.'

'But it's out there!' exclaimed a trembling

rabbit. 'I can feel it.'

Florence tutted loudly. 'Pull yourselves together,' she said. 'Help the Night Zookeeper and this giraffe inside!'

Will found himself being lifted off the ground and carried by lots of paws and feet and beaks and fins.

'Be careful of his leg,' instructed Florence.

'Doctor Florence, what's the Grip?' Will mumbled.

'Some animals have been going missing. The others think there's something in the lake kidnapping them,' she told him. 'They won't go near the water now.'

Will was about to ask another question, but he suddenly couldn't be bothered. His eyelids felt heavy and his vision narrowed. It was as if he were staring along a dark tunnel.

'Faster, everyone!' urged Riya, who was helping carry him.

'He has got it, hasn't he?' Will heard Florence ask Riya. 'Is it in his bag? Yes, here it is. Night Zookeeper, can you hear me?'

'Yes,' Will replied with great effort. 'I . . . hear you.'

'Night Zookeeper, I need your permission. I need to use your torch,' said Florence hurriedly. 'Can I use your torch? Night Zookeeper!'

Will's vision narrowed to a pinhole of light. 'Yes,' he whispered and then there was nothing but quiet and misty, grey darkness.

Sometime later, Will opened his eyes and Riya's face came into focus. She smiled down at him. 'Doctor Florence, he's awake,' she

said. Will blinked as the flamingo doctor appeared at the side of his bed.

'How are you feeling?' she asked.

'Hungry.'

'That's a good sign,' said Florence with a smile.

'Great, I'll fetch some palm toffees,' announced Riya and scooted off.

'Right, let's have a look at that leg,' said Doctor Florence, pulling the bed covers back carefully. Will lifted his head and peered down his

77

chest. His lower leg was still pale, but the long scratch was closed and already healing. Will wriggled his toes. His leg still ached, but the sharp pain was gone.

'It feels better,' he told Florence. 'Thank you. What did you do?'

'Normally, I use my healing feathers, but it's a slow cure. Luckily, you agreed to let me use this.' Florence held up Will's torch. 'This magical tool of yours drives away the darkness so much faster,' she said. 'Shall I show you?'

Will nodded. Florence held the torch close to his leg and pushed the switch.

The torch danced in her wing tips as the dazzling beam shot out, but Florence controlled it precisely. As she ran the beam along his wound, Will felt a soothing, warming glow in the muscle. His skin seemed to fill with light that glowed brighter and brighter and then spread right through his body. She switched off the torch. 'That's enough for now,' she said, wrapping a colourful bandage around his leg. 'It seems to be working well. And on your friend too.'

Will's eyes flew open. 'Sam!' he said. 'Where's Sam? Is he okay?'

'He's right there,' reassured Florence. Will

turned towards the bed next to him. In fact, the next door beds. Two of them had been pushed together to make enough room for Sam. The giraffe was fast asleep on his back. All four of his legs were suspended in the air by a contraption of poles, weights and wires. His shins were wrapped in neat bandages. Sam's tongue lolled from his mouth and there was a pool of dribble on the floor.

'Sam!' said Will in alarm. 'Why isn't he answering?'

'Don't worry,' said Florence softly. 'It looks worse than it is. He's recovering well. He needs to rest. And so do you, Night Zookeeper.'

'But I want to get up,' insisted Will. 'I want to help.' He tried to sit up in bed, but Florence spread an elegant pink wing and gently pushed him back down.

'Now then, even heroes need to rest sometimes,' she said.

'I'm not a hero,' exclaimed Will bitterly. 'Riya's the hero! She saved us. She should be the Night Zookeeper, not me!'

Florence reached down and touched his hand with a feather tip. 'It might not seem like it right now,' she said quietly, 'but you are made of the right stuff, Night Zookeeper.

Maji the Elephant chose you for a reason.'

Will shook his head. 'What reason? I'm no good at most things. Especially stuck in bed like this.'

Florence smiled down at him. 'But there you must stay to recover properly. Sometimes when

we are at our weakest, we learn how to be strong. And there is no shame in letting others pull us up when we are down.'

Will sighed. 'Doctor Florence, tell me more about the Grip. What does it look like? I want to understand what we're all facing.'

Florence Flamingo shook her head. 'I can't tell you, because no one's ever actually seen it.'

'But animals are going missing?' asked Will.

Florence nodded sadly. 'Every few days, there's another report. The most recent incident happened last time Captain Claw was here: Tabitha the Tortoise went for a stroll and just disappeared. I don't know what to believe, but that fog and the polluted water are making us scared of our own shadows.'

Will's leg twinged. 'Ouch,' he said.

'Okay, that's enough questions for now,' said Florence. 'Rest some more.'

'But I'm not tired,' Will argued.

'Rest!' said the doctor sternly.

Will stared out of the hospital window. A full moon was rising, bathing the silent room in glossy, silvery light. It seemed so peaceful, but Will kept thinking about what might be lurking in the lake. Was this Grip even real? And what was he supposed to do about it? Eventually, his eyes grew tired and he dropped into a sleep disturbed by vivid dreams.

Chapter Five

Will dreamt that he was sitting in front of his grandma's shed at the bottom of their garden. Grandma Rivers was telling one of her stories. 'And that was the moment the boy chose his future,' she was saying. 'The boy nodded and the heavy Mask was lowered into place, shutting out all the light and colour.'

Will couldn't really understand Grandma Rivers' story. In his dream, Sam suddenly poked his nose around the side of the shed. Will waved, but the young giraffe didn't look his way. His patchwork coat was faded and there was a dull sadness in his hooded eyes.

Grandma Rivers continued her strange tale. 'But, you see, it felt comforting to withdraw into the dark. It felt safe and easy and uncomplicated. The boy felt better inside the Mask. He didn't need to make an effort. He thought how much simpler it would be if everyone put on the Mask and just went along with things and didn't question or disagree.'

87

'Will,' said a voice he recognized. 'Will, wake up.' In his dream, Will searched around for Riya, but she wasn't on the garden wall. 'Will, wake up!' Riya's voice insisted.

The garden, Grandma Rivers, the shed and Sam all evaporated as Will's mind was dragged out of the dream. Will blinked as he sat up on the hospital bed. Riya was standing at his bedside. 'What's up?' Will asked, his voice croaky with sleep.

Riya stole a glance out of the window. 'You need to see this,' she replied. 'It's Captain Claw. She's down by the lake. I can hear her talking to someone, but I can't see anyone else. I think she's up to no good. Come quickly.' She looked down at his bandaged leg. 'Or, you know, as quickly as you can.'

'Help me up,' said Will. Will held Riya's

arm as he swung his legs out of bed. He put both feet flat on the floor and Riya pulled him upright. Will was relieved that his injured leg only felt a bit stiff, even with his weight on it. 'I feel so much better,' he announced brightly. 'Let's go then.'

Riya gave him an unimpressed look. 'Er, wake up, sleepyhead. Some shoes might help or you'll be straight back in here with burnt feet. And bring your things just in case.'

Will and Riya headed for the main door. Just as they got outside, Will suddenly stopped. 'Hang on,' he said.

'What's the matter? Is it your leg?'

'No, but where's Sam?' he asked with concern. 'His beds were empty.'

A long, dribbling tongue swept up the side of Will's face. 'Sam!' said Will, trying to sound annoyed. He wiped his cheek and ear with the cuff of his jacket.

Sam smiled down at him. 'Hey, Will, did you know it's good lick to be lucked by a giraffe? Oops, I mean, good luck to be licked!'

'Sure,' drawled Will, raising his eyebrows. 'Hey, your bandages are gone. That's great.'

'Look,' interrupted Riya. 'There she is. There's Claw.'

'Come on, Sam,' said Will. 'We've got some spying to do.'

'Listen. She's talking to someone,' Riya whispered. 'Can you hear what's she's saying?'

Will, Riya, and Sam were hiding in a grove of palm trees at the edge of the lake beach.

They watched as Captain
Claw paced up and down
the shoreline. The lioness
pilot seemed to be muttering
and growling to herself.

'Sam, can you turn
invisible?' asked Will quietly.
'Sneak up and listen?'

Sam looked
perplexed. 'You
mean, me,
a giraffe,
sneak up on
her, a lion? It's usually

the other way round!'

'Please, Sam, we really need your spying skills,' insisted Will. 'This is your moment.'

Sam chewed on his lower lip then sighed. 'Oh, alright. But I don't like it. First flying. Now this,' he complained. The young giraffe closed his eyes in concentration and disappeared from sight.

Invisible Sam tiptoed out of the palm grove and down the sand towards the prowling lioness. As he got closer, his legs and knees started quaking. At last he was close enough —too close!—so that he could make out some of what Captain Claw was muttering. 'I want to see you, Grip . . . Where are you? Come on . . . Show yourself!'

Sam couldn't believe his twitching ears. Claw was summoning the Grip! He had to report this terrible news to the others. He rushed to turn on the spot and his wobbling legs got in a terrible tangle. Sam stifled a cry as he lost his balance. Slowly, like a felled tree, the young giraffe toppled over with a thump.

Captain Claw jumped like a startled cat as a cloud of sand billowed up next to her. There was a flash of bright light as Sam lost concentration and became visible again. He was lying in a heap on the beach. He blinked the sand out of his long eyelashes. Claw crouched down and a low growl rattled in her throat. 'Skyscraper!' she snarled.

Sam swung his head round to shout to his friends in the trees. 'Will! Riya! Help! She's been calling the Grip. She's working with that monster!'

Will and Riya sprinted from the treeline down the beach. Captain Claw looked startled and backed away towards the water's edge. 'Hey, wait!' she said. 'That daft giraffe has got it all wrong. I'm not working with the Grip!'

'What were you saying?' demanded Riya.

'I was calling it,' admitted Claw. 'But only

because I want to fight it!'

'Fight the Grip? By yourself?' Will said suspiciously.

'Yes, by myself,' said Claw. 'I've been a coward. When you first saw me at the lake, I was trying to fly away. I've been running away too long. After I was hurt, every time I saw one of those robot spiders, I took off. But now I want to help the others here. Now I want to take on this Grip, whatever it is. You believe me, don't you, Night Zookeeper?'

Will was unsure. 'Riya, Sam, what do you think?' he called out.

Riya was frowning and said, 'Sounds suspicious to me.'

Sam, who had clambered to his feet, nodded his head. 'Riya's right. I heard her summon the Grip, Will. I was always taught to never trust a lion. Now I know why!'

Captain Claw roared at Sam. 'You've got it all wrong, you lanky llama,' she snarled.

Will stared at Captain Claw, trying to work out whether the lioness was telling the truth. He looked at the single scar on her nose and the scratch on his own leg throbbed. She had been hurt just like him. Will's instincts told him there was no way she could be betraying

98

them. 'She's telling the truth,' he said. Out of the corner of his eye, he noticed a ripple in the murky water behind her. The hairs on his arms stood up. 'Captain, get away from the water,' he blurted. Captain

Claw turned towards the lake just at the moment a long, metallic leg rose almost silently from the surface.

'The Grip!' cried Sam. 'I knew it. It's here to help her!'

A grey head broke the surface, the water cascading down past a single, crimson eye and

a set of shiny black fangs. A terrifying hiss filled the air.

'It's that Void,' said Riya. 'That Void must be the Grip!'

The Void gnashed its fangs together.

Clicker-clacker!

Captain Claw's whiskers were trembling, but she pulled her shoulders back and faced the robot monster. The Void rose further out of the water. It towered over the companions on the beach. Its head jerked as it cast its gaze from Claw, to Riya, to Sam, until its glowing eye settled on Will.

Clicker-clacker!

Clicker-clacker!

The Void struck out viciously at Will with one of its front legs. Its spiked foot swept down towards his head. Out of nowhere, Captain Claw sprang in front of Will and clubbed the Void's leg away with a powerful paw. 'Leave him alone,' she snarled. The Void hissed and stabbed at Will again. There was a screeching like the clash of swords as Claw deflected the robot's leg with her sharp claws. The lioness roared and the Void took a step backwards.

For a moment, Will thought the robot was retreating, but before anyone could react, a glistening metal cable shot out towards them. The cable wrapped around Claw's wrist and locked tight. The lioness looked at it in surprise and then she was jerked off her feet as the Void shot backwards into the lake. The Void submerged and accelerated, dragging Captain

Claw with incredible speed and force across the surface of the lake. The lioness' body rolled and bumped on the water as she roared and cried out for help. And then, within seconds, she had disappeared from sight into the bank of forbidding fog.

'Captain!' shouted Riya, but there was no reply.

Will started to rush towards the water, but Riya grabbed his arm. 'What are you doing? Be careful. The water's polluted, remember?'

Will turned his face towards her. His eyes were bright and moist, and his voice caught in his throat. 'We have to rescue her, Riya,' he insisted. 'She saved us all from that Void.' He glared at Sam, who looked down at his hooves.

'You're right,' replied Riya. 'We must, but how can we cross the lake? It's poisonous.' Will stared across the grey water towards the bank of churning fog. Riya put her head in her hands. 'There's got to be a way,' she said. 'Think, Will.'

'Hey, do you remember when we were stuck last time?' asked Will.

'When you were trapped in the forest, you mean? Oh, I see.'

Will nodded, reached into his bag and pulled out the glass sphere his grandma had given him. He pressed the Orb to his forehead.

Immediately, the dull interior of the glass globe glowed with swirling colours. Will closed his eyes and broken images began to swim behind his eyelids. Inside the Orb, colourful fragments began to gather and take shape. A complete image formed in Will's mind. His eyes snapped open and he examined the same image in the Orb. For a second, Will was bewildered. It was a duck! The object he had seen in his imagination and the one now in the Orb was a duck swimming across a pond. The colours in the Orb quickly faded and Will smiled to himself.

'Well? What did you see?' Sam asked.

'A duck,' replied Will. 'Swimming across a pond.'

'A duck?' echoed Riya in surprise.

'Ahhh, that's cute,' said Sam. 'But how can a duck help?'

'Come on, you guys!' said Will. 'Not just any duck. The Duck!'

'Le Canard!' exclaimed Riya.

Sam frowned. 'The seaplane? But it's kinda broken, Will,' he said. 'And even if we fix it, I'm not flying anywhere again!'

'We don't need to,' explained Will. 'The wings are broken, but the engine is still working. If we can get it floating again, we can drive it across the lake in no time at all.'

'That might just work,' nodded Riya.

'So, just to check, there will be no flying involved?' Sam asked. 'Just floating?'

'No flying, Sam, I promise,' confirmed Will.

'Alright, I'm in!' said the giraffe.

'Well, what are we waiting for?' said Riya and the three of them ran back up the beach towards the stranded seaplane.

Chapter Six

Will leaned out of the cockpit window.
'Ready . . . and push!' he shouted.
Sam lowered the top of his head and placed it
against the propeller. He planted his feet and
leant all his weight against the trapped plane.
'Go on!' encouraged Will. The wings creaked
and groaned as they ground against the palm
trees.

'You can do it, Sam!' shouted Riya out of the other window.

Sam strained again, but the seaplane barely moved an inch: the smashed wings were well and truly wedged in the two trees. Sam backed off and gasped for breath. 'It's no good,' he said miserably. 'I'm not strong enough.'

'No, but maybe we all are,' came a voice. Florence Flamingo fluttered to the ground next to him. And then between the trees appeared a huge crowd. The tapir, the fox, all the band members, and many others, even a chicken on crutches, had all left the safety of the hospital. 'We saw everything from the window,' said Florence. 'We saw how brave Captain Claw was. We have to help you save her.'

Will beamed down at them from the cockpit. 'Thank you, Florence,' he said.

'Well, everyone, let's get this duck back on the pond!' Florence cried. The animals rushed to brace themselves against the plane's floats, struts, and nose. 'Push!' she bellowed.

The plane juddered backwards with a screech of metal as the wings were finally ripped loose from the trees.

'Look out!' shouted Riya as both wings sheared off completely and thumped down on the sand. Without the weight of the wings, the seaplane was much easier to push. It slid smoothly down the slope on its floats until it entered the water tail first. The crowd of animals cheered and clapped on the beach. There was a whirl of pink feathers as Florence took to the air and touched down lightly on the seaplane's wing.

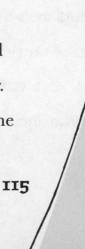

'Room for one more?' she asked.

Will nodded and opened the door. 'Welcome aboard,' he

115

said with a smile and turned towards the instruments panel.

'I guess I'm on the roof again,' said Sam apprehensively.

'Hurry up, Sam. Get on,' called out Riya, closing the doors and windows. 'And make sure you don't get splashed.'

Will punched the ignition and the engine spluttered into life. Using the pedals to turn the rudder, Will eased the throttle open and turned the seaplane's nose to face the bank of dense fog on the far side of the lake.

The seaplane was rocketing across the lake. It

was a wild ride. The cockpit rattled and shook as Le Canard bumped and banged on its floats over the surface.

Florence was standing just behind the pilots' seats. She had to talk loudly to make herself heard over the roar of the engine. 'I knew it!' she cursed. 'I knew the others were wrong about the Grip. It was a Void all along!'

'Not just any old Void,' said Riya. 'A huge one that can swim underwater.'

'A Void all the same,' the flamingo replied. 'And Voids can be defeated. They're empty shells. Mindless robots that just follow orders.'

'Orders? Whose orders?' asked Will in surprise.

'His orders. The orders of Lord Nulth,' Florence said. 'His forces are attacking animals across the Night Zoo. I never thought the Voids would make it this far into the Fire Desert, but it seems we've had one living right under our noses, kidnapping those poor animals!'

'But what does this Lord Nulth want with them?' asked Will. 'What does he do to them?'

'I'm sorry, but that I don't know,' sighed Florence. 'But we're all hoping that you'll find out and stop him.'

Will swallowed hard. It was terrifying enough to fight the Voids, but now it seemed there was a greater threat: someone capable of controlling an army of robots; someone terrifying and kidnapping animals across the Night Zoo; someone he was supposed to stop! He was about to protest when there was a loud knocking on the cockpit ceiling.

'Knock, knock,' shouted Sam.

'Yes, Sam?' replied Riya.

'No, knock, knock!' repeated the giraffe.

Riya rolled her eyes. 'OK, who's there?'

'A duck goes.'

'A duck goes who?'

'No, Riya, an owl goes who. A duck goes quack!' giggled Sam. 'Geddit? Quack!'

'Did you want something?' said Riya, trying not to smile.

'Well, the good news is I'm still dry. The bad news is my ossicones are picking something up,' replied the giraffe. 'Better slow down.'

Will looked through the windscreen. They were closing in on the fog rapidly. Will throttled

back the engine and the
seaplane's floats settled
lower in the water as it
slowed.

'It must be the Void,'
said Riya. She looked
solemnly at the fog. 'It's in
there somewhere.'

Will opened the window and called
up to Sam quietly, 'Take us towards it. Call out
directions.'

Sam bent his head down to the window.
'Really?' he said doubtfully. 'Okaaay, if
you're sure.'

'I'm sure,' Will replied firmly. 'Guide us through this fog.'

Will reduced the power further until the propeller was just turning over. The seaplane slowed to a crawl. The cockpit suddenly went almost dark as the seaplane drifted into the fog. 'Left a bit,' called out Sam in a loud whisper. 'Straight . . . straight . . . now, right.' Will shivered: cold mist was seeping in through the windows. 'Stop!' hissed Sam. 'We're here.'

Will quickly turned off the engine. The propeller jerked to a halt. Suddenly, the fog thinned a little and a sandy beach appeared dead ahead of them. The seaplane slid silently across the shallows and stopped with a gentle bump against the shoreline. Florence opened the door and hopped onto the sand with a flap of her wings. Will and Riya climbed down onto the floats and leapt onto the sand. As he landed, Will's injured leg buckled beneath him. He winced in pain.

'Take it easy,' warned Florence. 'It will take some time to heal properly.'

Will looked around warily. The air was still cool in the thin mist, but the atmosphere felt oppressive. The desert felt even more desolate and empty, but also full of unseen threats. Sam stood next to him, scanning the air with his ossicones.

'Which way now?' Will asked.

Sam shook his head. 'I'm not sure,' he whispered. 'The signal's much fainter now.'

'Don't worry. I think I know,' announced Riya grimly. 'Look.' She was pointing at the ground. The sand was splattered with shiny tar. 'And there. And there,' Riya added. There was a trail of the Void Gunk leading away up the beach towards a high dune.

'Let's follow it,' said Will. 'It's our only chance of finding Captain Claw.'

Crouching low to the ground, they followed the trail of Void Gunk up to the crest of the dune. Will dropped down onto his belly and peeked over the other side. It was a grim spectacle. Messy heaps of jagged metal lay all around. Black tar lay in glossy puddles around each pile. There was strong smell of oil and smoke.

'What is all this?' whispered Florence.

'Looks like some kind of junkyard,' said Will.

'Whatever it is, it's a big operation, Will. We need to be very careful,' said Riya.

'Sam, can you sense anything?' asked Will. 'Any sign of the Void?'

'No, nothing at the moment. My ossicones are as quiet as an eskimouse,' he replied.

'Good, we need to take a closer look,' said Will.

They dropped over the ridge and down towards the stinking, oily workshop. Will examined one of the piles of metal. Up close, it was clear that this was the same black and grey metal that the Voids were made from. He spotted a smaller piece of metal lying in some tar. It was shaped like a bird's wing. They moved on to the next pile. Will noticed another object. He picked it up carefully.

'What have you found?' asked Riya.

Will examined it. He could think of no other way to describe it. 'It looks like a helmet, but for a rabbit.'

'What is happening here?' asked Florence anxiously.

'Will!' cried Sam suddenly. 'I've found them! They're over here!'

Will, Riya, and Florence dashed around a pile of junk and saw them too. There was a row of sturdy cages of different dimensions, each secured with a padlock. Will looked from cage to cage: there was a porcupine, a baboon, a giant tortoise, a hawk, and more. Finally, his eyes fell upon the lioness pilot, who was lying with her chin on her paws. Here were Captain Claw and all the other kidnapped animals.

Will rushed forwards and knelt by her cage. 'Captain,' he said. 'I'm so pleased we found you.' Captain Claw glanced round at him. Her eyes looked pale grey, not amber. At first Will thought it was a trick of the misty light,

but then he noticed her coat was grey too. Even the gold hoops in her ears had faded. 'Captain?' Will said with a frown. 'It's me. Will, the Night Zookeeper.' Claw blinked. She didn't seemed at all bothered to see him. In fact, she didn't even seem to recognize him. Claw yawned and looked away. Will jumped up and checked some of the other animals. They were all the same: grey, listless, and indifferent.

'What's the matter with them?' he asked, disheartened.

Florence said, 'Here's my diagnosis. It must

be the cages. The metal must be affecting them, like the lake water affected Sam and your wound affected you.'

'We need to get them out,' urged Riya.

Will was one step ahead of her. He already had his torch in his hand.

'This might not work on that Void, but it will work on these cages,' he said and aimed the torch at the padlock on Claw's cage. He held down the button, and the bright beam filled the inside of the lock, which then smashed apart. The cage door swung open. 'Help her out,' he ordered. 'I'll break the other locks.'

Will worked as fast as he could, blasting

away the padlocks as Riya, Sam, and Florence dragged each sluggish animal free from its cage. When the last lock was destroyed, Will half-ran, half-hobbled on his aching leg back to Captain Claw. The lioness was back on her feet. She smiled at Will and then a look of terror flashed across her amber eyes. There was a powerful hiss and screech of metal. Will swivelled round on the spot. The air above the junkyard was glowing red, and then the giant Void stepped into view.

Chapter Seven

Clicker-clacker!

The Void gnashed its fangs in fury as it noticed all the open cages. It reared up on its back legs and spurted sticky tar directly at Will. He scrambled out of the way and pointed the torch at the Void.

'Stay back!' he shouted, trying to sound threatening.

The Void glared at Will, hissed and lunged at him. A spiked foot swished over his head, missing his cap by inches. Will pushed the switch and aimed the beam at the Void's leg.

Again, it had no real effect.

Clicker-clacker!

The Void stepped confidently towards him, its red eye glowing with menace. Will backed away, keeping his eyes firmly on the Void. He bumped into something cold and hard. He glanced back only to realize that he had backed himself into a corner amongst a pile of metal. His heart thundered in his chest as the Void gnashed its fangs and raised a spiked foot. Will's injured leg ached. He suddenly felt like hiding underneath the pile of metal and not coming out. It was no good. He couldn't do it. No one could stop such a huge Void.

There was a flash of neon pink above the Void. 'Get away!' shouted Florence Flamingo. 'I'll distract it!' She spread her wings and pointed the tips to the sky. She then pirouetted in the air, twirling faster and faster until she was just a blur. She looked like a giant pink candyfloss floating in the grey sky. The Void broke off its attack, mesmerized by the spinning flamingo. 'Can't catch me,' Florence taunted above its head. The Void hissed and swiped at her, but she flew a little higher.

Will searched for an escape route. There was nothing he could do here. It was better to retreat and get to safety. Then he saw Riya and Sam helping the other animals, who were either still weak or now terrified. He flushed with shame. His friends weren't thinking of themselves. They weren't full of doubts. They were simply helping the most vulnerable. A spasm of pain ran up from Will's leg, but he ignored it. He wasn't going to run away anywhere.

The Void swiped at Florence again, who was now darting left and right to avoid its attacks. She

climbed

higher and

the Void heaved itself up onto its back

legs. Will looked at the rearing robot

and tried to clear his mind. He didn't

have time to use the Orb. 'Think,' he

commanded himself through gritted teeth.

And that's when he saw it. There was something

strange about the Void's underbelly: dark tar

was dripping from a gap between its armoured

plates. He remembered how a plate of armour

had been knocked off by the seaplane's tail.

'It's still damaged!' Will whispered to himself.

The Void might have a weak spot after all! Remembering what the torch had done to the padlocks, he re-gripped it in his hand.

The Void was swaying left and right, viciously swiping at Florence. She was still flitting just out of reach, but she seemed to be reacting more slowly. Will clenched his jaw. He knew he only had one shot at this while the Void's underbelly was exposed. And he needed to get closer for maximum effect. Will fought to control his breathing and steady his shaking legs. Florence shrieked as a spiked foot brushed one of her wings. NOW! Will rushed forward, sprinting towards the Void. His instincts

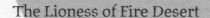

screamed at him to turn around. Instead, he dropped to the ground, thrusting his feet out in front of him. As he slid on his back beneath the looming Void, he aimed and pressed the button.

There was a blinding flash of colourful light. The giant Void suddenly stood paralysed on its rear legs. Will had aimed perfectly. The light from his torch was flooding into the Void through the gap in its armour. Smoke billowed and sparks flew out of its belly. Another armoured plate dropped off and the Void's joints began to glow red. Its whole body began to creak and expand, just like the padlocks. Sensing what was about to happen, Florence dived out of the way behind the cages, Riya leapt behind some junk and Sam broke into a gallop. The colourful light began to leak from the Void's joints as the pressure built. Its wide red eye turned white and then there was a deafening blast. Will dropped to his knees and covered his head as black powder and chunks of Void metal rained down from a rainbow in the sky. The explosion echoed through the dunes and then there was silence. Not a hiss to be heard.

Will hardly dared to open his eyes. He stood up and stepped forwards cautiously. Riya popped up close by. 'Did you do it?' she asked. 'Did you destroy it?'

Florence stepped out from behind the cages. 'It's gone!' she exclaimed. 'You did it, Night Zookeeper!' Will looked around, really hoping that she was right. He bumped his toe on something. At his feet lay a smoking metal tube. It was one of the Void's fangs! Will gasped as colour flooded back into the junkyard. The sand became honey-golden and the mist disappeared to reveal a cloudless sky scattered with silver stars. Small, bright flowers popped up through the sand.

Will rushed over to the other animals. Their coats and feathers were flushing with colour, driving out the grey. Captain Claw was smiling, her eyes were a sparkling amber colour again and her coat was glossy and golden.

'You could have run,' the lioness said to Will, 'but you saved us all.'

'Believe me, I thought about it,' admitted Will.

Florence put a long, pink wing around Will's shoulders. 'You did a great job today, Night Zookeeper,' she said. Will didn't respond: he was deep in thought. 'What is it?' the flamingo asked.

'Florence, you told me that

we learn how to be strong when we are at our weakest,' said Will. 'I'm not sure that's true.'

Florence looked at him quizzically with her sharp eyes. 'What do you mean?'

'I think it's when others are at their weakest that we find that strength inside us,' explained Will.

Florence nodded and smiled. 'You know, I think you just might just be right, Night Zookeeper.'

Will led his friends and all the others over the dunes back towards the seaplane. Some of the animals were still slow and confused, and

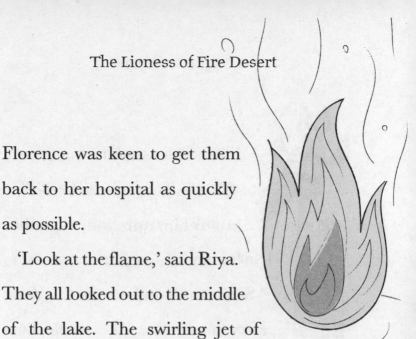

Florence was keen to get them back to her hospital as quickly as possible.

'Look at the flame,' said Riya. They all looked out to the middle of the lake. The swirling jet of flame was pink again.

'And the lake!' added Sam. The water in the shallows was crystal clear.

Riya turned to Captain Claw. 'How are we going to get everyone on board, Captain?'

'That's a good question,' she replied.

Sam grinned. 'Don't worry, Captain. Now the lake's clean again, I've got a great idea,' he said.

The lioness glared at Sam. 'Watch it, Spaghetti Legs. You think I trust your opinion? Don't imagine I've forgiven you yet.'

Sam look embarrassed. 'Yeah, sorry about that, the whole lion-giraffe trust thing,' he replied. 'No hard feelings?'

'No hard feelings!' growled Claw in disbelief. 'I tell you one thing: you can forget riding on my plane again.'

'I know!' cried Sam. 'That's the whole point.'

Le Canard shot across the lake towards Florence's hospital. Inside, Captain Claw was sitting at the controls with Riya as her co-pilot. In the back, Will was helping Florence look after the smaller animals. Outside, hanging onto the tail, was Sam. 'Wheee!' he cried, as he water-skied on his back legs behind the plane. And attached to Sam were the other animals. The baboon was clamped to his leg, the giant tortoise to his back, and clinging to his ossicones was the porcupine, its quills sticking up in the air in shock. 'Wheee! Faster, faster,' Sam shouted.

Will smiled out of the window at him. 'You

make a great life raft, Sam,' he called out.

'More like a life-giraft!' said Sam. 'Geddit? Life-giraffe-t?'

As the seaplane taxied to a halt by the shore, the band struck up a merry tune. Captain Claw cut off the engine and the sound of cheering and clapping filled the air. Will opened the door and the applause grew even warmer.

'Hooray for the Night Zookeeper!' the animals shouted. 'Hooray for Doctor Florence!'

Will climbed down onto the beach. He waved his hands to quieten the cheering crowd. The band stopped playing and everyone listened.

Will felt uncomfortable with all those eyes on him, but he needed to say something. 'Hi,' he said.

'Hi,' chorused the crowd.

'I just wanted to say that the Void is gone,' he began. The crowd cheered wildly. 'But, but you're not safe yet!' he had to shout. The crowd stopped cheering. 'It seems that Lord Nulth's forces are spreading across the Night Zoo.' The crowd murmured unhappily. 'You must stay alert. The Grip never existed. The Void tricked you and I expect Lord Nulth will try to trick you again. The Grip was fake but the danger is real.' The crowd started to grumble loudly.

Sam whispered in Will's ear, 'Er, where are you going with this?'

Will ignored him. 'What I'm trying to say,' he continued, 'is that whatever threat you face, wherever some monster next appears, me and my friends will defend you. I promise you that. You can count on me, the Night Zookeeper!'

A huge cheer filled the desert air. Animals rushed forwards, and Will found himself lifted off his feet and carried on their shoulders. Laughing, he glanced round to see Riya, Florence, and Captain Claw being held aloft too. 'They're all heroes! Hooray for the heroes!' the animals chanted.

The giant tortoise looked up at Sam. 'You're my hero,' she said. 'Would you like me to carry you?'

'Thanks, why not?' replied Sam. 'That's very kind of you.' He clambered onto her broad shell and she plodded slowly after the others. 'Hmm, not quite as exciting as water-skiing,' Sam muttered to himself.

Later, as the celebrations were winding down, Will spotted Captain Claw away down the beach by the palm trees. She was inspecting the seaplane's wings. Will left the others and wandered over.

'Sorry for all this damage,' said Will, looking at the battered wings.

Claw smiled. 'There's no need for that,'  she said. 'I can fix Le Canard. It will take a few weeks, but there are plenty of spare parts on the other side of the Great

Pink Lake. I was just about to set off over there.' Captain Claw paused and fixed Will with her piercing, amber eyes. 'Listen, I can never thank you enough, Night Zookeeper,' she said. 'You trusted me when I hardly trusted myself. Then you rescued me. But it is the first of those things I will remember longest. Well, say goodbye to the others for me, even that clumsy leaf-muncher.'

Will shook the lioness' paw and then she bounded into the cockpit of the seaplane. The engine roared into life. Le Canard turned away and accelerated across the water. Will was waving as Doctor Florence landed gracefully next to him. She looked serious.

'What's the matter?' he asked. 'What's happened?'

'We have some new patients,' said Florence. 'They arrived from Igloo City when we were away. I've never seen sickness like it. The city must be in grave danger.'

Will nodded. 'I understand,' he said. He glanced over at the partying animals. He wished for a moment that he could stay a little longer, but he had made a promise. 'Please could you ask Riya and Sam to join me?' he said.

Florence flapped her wings and returned to the party. Will took the torch out of his bag. Pointing it at the clear desert sky, he pressed the button. The torch throbbed in his hand as the beam carved out another huge eternity symbol in the air. Riya and Sam came to stand next to Will. Snow-white light glimmered through the portal and a flurry of snowflakes drifted onto the sand.

'Ready?' asked Will.

Riya nodded. 'Now that Void's gone, it looks like things are happier here for now,' she said. 'You did an amazing job, Will.'

'We did an amazing job,' he corrected her.

Sam was eyeing the falling snow suspiciously. 'Wow, someone through there has got really bad dandruff,' he said.

Riya laughed. 'That's snow, Sam,' she said. 'You have seen snow before, right?'

A flake landed on the young giraffe's nose. He peered down his snout at it in surprise. 'Ooh, it's cold!' he exclaimed. 'I mean, of course it's cold. Everyone knows that.'

'So where are we going next?' Riya asked.

'Igloo City,' said Will.

'Sounds freezing,' said Riya.

'Great! I just got used to the heat,' complained Sam.

The Lioness of Fire Desert

With the Fire Desert free from the Grip, Will
and his two companions stepped through the
magical portal and into their next adventure.

Joshua Davidson

By night, Joshua Davidson is the head Night Zookeeper. He works in the Night Zoo and cares for many magical animals such as Purple Octocows and Banana Hedgehogs. During his nightly rounds he enjoys playing memory games with the Time-Travelling Elephant and hide-and-seek with the Spying Giraffes. Sadly, he is yet to win a single game in either contest.

By day, he is an author, artist, game designer, and tech entrepreneur. He came up with the idea for nightzookeeper.com, a website where anyone can draw animals and write stories about them, whilst studying an MA in Digital Art at Norwich University of the Arts.

Josh introduced the Night Zoo to Paul, Buzz, Phil, and Sam and together they built the Night Zookeeper website. It has since been nominated for a BAFTA, won a London Book Fair award, and is currently used in thousands of schools across the world to inspire amazing creative writing.

Buzz Burman

Buzz studied graphic design in Norwich, England where he met Night Zookeeper Josh. Many years later, Josh brought Buzz to the gates of the Night Zoo. Ever since then he has been the regular painter and decorator in the zoo. He draws on his gigantic imagination to care for the animals there and to explore new parts of the world!

By day, Buzz is a designer and illustrator with a love of clever ideas. As well as drawing what the animals look like in this book, he also designed the cover, the Night Zookeeper website, and Night Zookeeper logo!

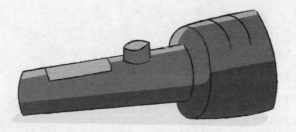

Write your own adventure story

At nightzookeeper.com you can test your powers of imagination and create your own Night Zookeeper adventures. Just as William and Maddier16 have done in these stories.

Why Do Birds Sing?
By William, Year 5, Singapore

'Quick!!!' shouted the birds. 'It's happening!' And out of his egg, hatched a new parrot. 'I'm going to call you 'Squawk,'' she said.

Squawk had been living with his parents in the tall pine tree for eight years. He had learnt many things in the forest like how to write, draw and fly. One great thing about him, is that

Squawk had the prettiest multicoloured feathers of all birds. They were beautiful.

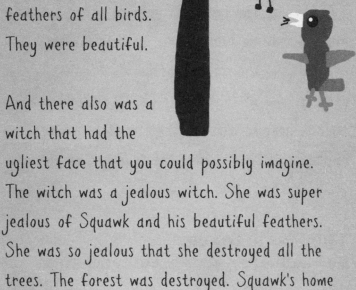

And there also was a witch that had the ugliest face that you could possibly imagine. The witch was a jealous witch. She was super jealous of Squawk and his beautiful feathers. She was so jealous that she destroyed all the trees. The forest was destroyed. Squawk's home was destroyed.

The forest was gone. The birds had nowhere to live. He was lying there next to the ruins of the tall pine tree. To cheer himself and to say sorry to the forest, he sang a song. Then suddenly a leaf started growing. So Squawk sang again.

It worked! The tree was growing with the music! Soon he told the entire bird village to sing until their tree was grown. Finally, after a long while, the forest was rebuilt and Squawk became a hero! That, reader, is why birds sing, to grow their tree every time the witch destroys it.

The Magic Foxes
By Maddier16, Year 2, United States

Once there was a girl named Lily. She had long brown hair pulled back in a ponytail. She believed in magic. One day Lily was selling cakes in the garden. Suddenly the King's men came and announced that he had made a magical animal

Ma gic!

detector. It could sense magic animals and capture them. Lily heard about it and went to a pond. She wanted to be alone.

Then, out of nowhere a family of foxes appeared. They explained that they were magical foxes and could turn invisible. Lily told them the news about what the King's men had said. The foxes had to hide. Their names were Sara, Fluffy, and Cuddles. Lily said they should go to a lake. It would be the safest place. While Lily was explaining the plan to Sara and Cuddles, Fluffy turned invisible and climbed inside Lily's basket.

The two foxes went off to find the lake. Then Lily saw a person. She reached in her basket to give the person a treat. But all she felt was fluffy stuff. She pulled it out and Fluffy appeared. 'Fluffy, what are you doing here?'

'I smelled something good so I climbed in. I kind of ate it all. Sorry.'

'That's OK. But first we need to get you to the lake and destroy that machine.'

On the way to the lake they found a dragon kite. 'Maybe we can distract the knights and destroy the machine,' said Fluffy.

'Okay,' said Lily.

'Where is it?'

'I think it was by the lake.'

'Well let's go find it,' said Lily.

So off they went to the lake. They got the dragon kite and a candle to make it look like the dragon was breathing fire. Then they hung it up. The knights saw this and went chasing it. While the knights were busy chasing the dragon, Fluffy turned invisible and bit the machine until it broke. When the knights realized they were tricked, they went home very sad. Lily took Fluffy home and said goodbye, but Cuddles said, 'Take this necklace. It has the power to make you invisible.'

'Thank you for rescuing our sister.'

'You are welcome,' said Lily.

How to write your own adventure story

Now it's your turn to try some creative writing.
Use these steps to help you create your own
exciting adventure story.

STEP 1

The Beginning: Describe your lead character.
Likes – Dislikes – What makes this animal special?

The lead character in my story is called the
Penguin Professor. He loves reading books,
drinking hot chocolate, and wearing his favourite
red scarf wherever he goes!

STEP 2

The Beginning: Describe your opening setting.
Where does your character live?

My story takes place in Igloo City. This is
an incredibly cold place filled with thousands
of ice homes for a great many penguins. A
giant ice palace towers above all the other
igloos in the city.

STEP 3

The Middle: What problem does your character face?

Does something happen to your character? What changes in their world?

Some of the igloos in the city begin to melt because of rising temperatures in the Night Zoo. The Penguin Professor volunteers to help solve this disastrous problem!

STEP 4

The Middle: Does your character go on an adventure to solve their problem?

Where does your character go? What happens to them along the way?

The Penguin Professor begins his journey to the Fire Desert, as he believes the heat from the desert may be the cause of the problem. On his way, he meets Night Zookeeper Will and explains all about what's happening in Igloo City.

STEP 5

The End: How will your story end? Will it have a happy, sad, or cliffhanger ending?

How has the world changed?
What did your animal learn?

The Night Zookeeper and Penguin Professor discover a secret in the Fire Desert that helps them to prevent rising temperatures in Igloo City. All the penguins thank the heroes! Before the story ends, a shooting star flies across the sky and strikes the Penguin Professor's igloo . . .

The Zoo Needs You!

Continue your adventure on
nightzookeeper.com

Create your own magical animals

Defeat
evil Voids

Rescue Sam the Spying Giraffe

Night Zookeeper uses storytelling and technology to encourage creativity and imagination. Our magical stories inspire traditional creative play and develop reading, writing, and drawing skills.

We believe in fairness and offer free digital education products to all children around the world.

Thank you for buying this book and supporting our mission.

Visit **nightzookeeper.com** for more information.

The adventure
continues in . . .

NIGHT ZOO KEEPER

The Penguins of
Igloo City

Will, Sam, and Riya have stepped through the magical portal and are travelling deep into the heart of the eerie Igloo City . . .

A few minutes later, Sam came to a slippery stop and peered into the semi-darkness over the igloos. 'There's something up ahead,' he whispered. 'Lots of black blobs, standing like soldiers on parade.'

Will clenched his jaw. It didn't sound like Voids, so what new enemy was this? 'Sam, get your head down and let's take a closer look,' he said.

They weaved between a few more igloos and suddenly found themselves in a huge town square. Will sighed with relief. The animals hadn't run away. They were all here! There were hundreds of penguins, all standing in neat rows and staring up at a raised ice platform. At the end of each row of penguins stood a wolf wearing a metal helmet with a blade like a short mohican. The wolves were watching the penguins with their piercing yellow eyes.

'This is weird. What are they all doing?' asked Riya suspiciously.

'I'm not sure about this, Will,' Sam said. 'My ossicones are still jingle-jangling.'

'Yeah, maybe we shouldn't just go barging in,' added Riya.

Will gave her a look of disbelief. 'I never thought I'd hear you say that,' he said. 'Come on, you two. We've found everyone and I promised to help; that's what matters. Let's find who's in charge.' He strode forwards. 'Hey, hi everyone!'

As they reached the first row of penguins, a ripple of noise passed through the crowd. Some of the penguins squawked and flapped their little wings excitedly. Their whispers grew louder and louder.

'It's him!' exclaimed one. 'The Night Zookeeper.'

'Look at his beautiful coat,' said another.

The penguins broke ranks and began to close in on him. Will was surprised that some of them were nearly as tall as he was. He heard one of the wolves howl and others barking and growling.

'The badge on his cap is so shiny,' said another voice. The penguins were jostling Will now. 'We'd never be allowed a cap like that!'

Will was beginning to feel trapped as black

and white bodies bumped into each other and him. 'Hey, wait a minute,' he protested. He glanced over his shoulder to see that Riya and Sam were also both being mobbed by the excited penguins. 'Hey, back off, Waddles!' he heard Riya say.

Suddenly, Will felt something grab his collar. He tried to twist away, but there was a rush of air and he was lifted off his feet. 'Thanks, Sam,' he called out, thinking the young giraffe had come to his rescue again. But as he rose higher, to his surprise, he swung round and spotted Sam still in the crowd of penguins. There was a beating of powerful wings above him, and Will found his feet touch down on top of the ice platform. Now the penguins were pointing up at him, all shouting and squawking loudly. The helmeted wolves were snapping at them, trying to restore some order. Will turned to see who had carried him up through the air. Next to him, there was a large, white owl wearing a beautiful, silver breastplate. She raised one wing tip into the cold air. Immediately, the crowd fell silent and the penguins shuffled hurriedly back into line. Will couldn't help being impressed. She reminded him of one of his teachers, Mrs

Barnes, who could silence a school assembly with a single stare. This owl was definitely in charge. A little nervously, Will stretched out a hand. 'How do you do?' he said, as politely as he could.

The owl turned her neck to look at him with round, orange eyes. Her stare was neither friendly nor unfriendly, but it was so intense that Will dropped his gaze. Then she blinked and smiled. 'Welcome, Night Zookeeper,' she said. 'My name is Circles. I am the Mayor of Igloo City. It's a pleasure to meet you.' She held out her wing and Will shook it enthusiastically.

'You too,' he said.

Circles turned to face the crowd below. 'Citizens of Igloo City!' she boomed. 'This is indeed a joyful day. Help has arrived in our darkest hour. Friends, I present to you . . . our Night Zookeeper!' Circles flung out a wing towards Will. The huge crowd of penguins cheered and clapped their flippers together as one. Even the wolves threw back their heads and howled their approval. Will felt his cheeks burning with so many eyes on him. 'Oh, happy times!' cried Circles. 'At last, the gates shall soon be opened!' The crowd cheered even louder and in places the penguins began to sing and dance.

A flash of anger passed across Circles' face.
Her chest heaved under her armoured
breastplate as she took a deep breath and
bellowed, 'Stop! Have you forgotten our rules
so quickly? We're not safe yet.' Again,
the crowd fell instantly still and silent.
'Remember: you must not attract attention!'
the owl berated the audience. 'No singing!
No dancing! These rules are for your
own good! Now return to your homes,
citizens.' Will watched as the penguins began
to shuffle off into the lanes, muttering and
whispering.

'Come, Night Zookeeper,' said Circles, staring directly at him again. 'We have much to discuss.'

Ready for more great stories?